Anthony Ant
Saves the Day

Anthony Ant
Saves the Day

By Lauren St John

Illustrated by Tamara Anegon

Orion
Children's Books

First published in Great Britain in 2015
by Orion Children's Books
a division of the Orion Publishing Group Ltd
Orion House
5 Upper Saint Martin's Lane
London WC2H 9EA
An Hachette UK Company

1 3 5 7 9 10 8 6 4 2

The Orion Publishing Group's policy is to use papers that are natural,
renewable and recyclable products and made from wood grown in
sustainable forests. The logging and manufacturing processes are expected
to conform to the environmental regulations of the country of origin.

ISBN 978 1 4440 0804 3

A catalogue record for this book is available from the British Library.

Printed and bound in China

www.orionbooks.co.uk

Contents

Chapter One

Every day Anthony Ant had to battle to move around the jungle.

The other animals were always nearly knocking him over or crushing him.

One morning, a clumsy butterfly
bashed him with her wing.

Anthony flew off a flower petal
and crashed to the ground.

"Watch where you're going!" he
cried, but she didn't hear him.
He barely came up to her knees.

With a flap of her wings, she blew
him off his feet and was gone.

"I hate being small," he told
his mum that night. "Nobody
notices me."

"Ants might be tiny but we're very important," said his mum. "When we work together, we can move mountains."

Anthony wasn't sure. "There are no ant heroes in books or on TV."

Chapter Two

Next morning Anthony decided to become the first ant hero in the history of the world.

While he was deciding how to go about it, a chameleon spotted him.

"Breakfast!" cried
the chameleon.

Then his tongue shot out and grabbed Anthony.

In one more second, Anthony
would be gone!

"Stop!!!"

The chameleon blinked and spat him out. "Excuse me?"

"You can't eat me,"
said Anthony.

"Of course I can eat you," said the chameleon. "I can't think of anything I'd enjoy more.

You're **young**.

You're **juicy**.

You'll be
delicious.

Just close your eyes. It'll be over in a second."

"No!" yelled Anthony.
The chameleon rolled his
eyes. "What's wrong now?"

"You can't eat me because I'm going to be a hero," Anthony said quietly.

The chameleon laughed so
hard that Anthony was shaken
all over.

"Don't be silly. Whoever
heard of an ant hero?

Jaguars and elephants can be heroes.

Even rabbits occasionally save the day. But not ants."

He licked his lips.

"Ants are meant to be squashed or eaten."

Chapter Three

A tear rolled down Anthony's face.

"It's not fair. Why was I born
a measly peasly ant? If I was as
big as an elephant, I could do
anything."

"Don't cry," said the chameleon.
"Okay, I won't eat you. Will
that make you happy?"

"Yes," said Anthony. "But what would **really** make me happy is if I could be a hero."

The chameleon thought hard.

"You don't have to be big to be a hero. You just have to be tall."
"Aren't they the same thing?"

"Not in the least. To be tall, all
you have to do is climb up high."
He pointed at a tree. It was so
huge that Anthony's neck hurt as
he tried to see the top.

"If you climbed up there, you'd be the tallest ant on earth," the chameleon said. "If you climbed up there, you'd be a giant."

Chapter Four

Anthony started climbing right
away.

He was feeling quite tired when
the clumsy butterfly bumped into
the tree trunk beside him.

"Oops," she said, rubbing her
head.

"Stay away from me," cried Anthony. "Yesterday you knocked me into the dirt."

She looked at him
in surprise. "Did I? Sorry.
I don't see very well
without my glasses."

47

"Are these your glasses?" said
Anthony, finding them under
a flower.

She took them from him with a
squeak of joy. "Gosh, I can see
again. You're just an ant. What
are you doing up here?"

"I'm trying to be tall so I can be a hero," Anthony said.

"That's easy," the butterfly told him, "Just hop on my wing and I'll give you a ride."

Soon Anthony was soaring
through the air. Flying was the
best feeling on earth. He saw
a snake, a spider monkey and
even a jaguar.

The butterfly landed halfway up
the tree. There was more climbing
to do, but a friendly parrot let
Anthony sit on
her back.

In no time at all, he was at the
top of the tallest tree in the
whole jungle. He was almost in
the clouds.

The view was amazing.
Anthony could see rivers and
mountains and lots of trees.

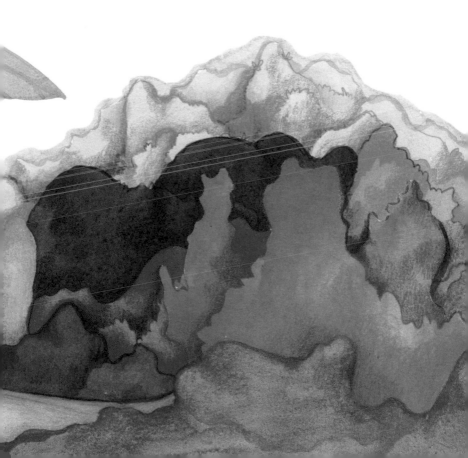

He felt like a giant, but he still didn't feel like a hero.

Chapter Five

He was about to climb down when, far away, he saw a bulldozer.

His mum had told him all about them. Men came in bulldozers and chopped down the trees. They killed the animals or took them away to zoos.

Bulldozers were bad!

Anthony took a deep breath. "Help!" he yelled at the top of his voice. "Mum! Dad! HELP!! The bulldozers are coming."

The parrots flew down to tell
the jaguar,

who told
the monkeys,
who told the
anaconda.

The butterfly told the ants.
"Come on everyone," yelled
Anthony's dad. "The bulldozers
are coming. Let's march."

Millions of tiny ants stood
side by side until it looked
as if a thick black carpet
was covering the
jungle floor.

Behind them came beetles,
butterflies and frogs. The
monkeys, jaguar and the hissing
anaconda followed.

65

Anthony was given a lift to the ground by the parrot and marched beside his dad.

The ants swarmed through the jungle.

They crossed a bridge over
a river full of fish with sharp
teeth.

They climbed a small
mountain.

When they saw the men with their bulldozers, they crawled up their trouser legs and bit them all over.

The parrots pecked their ears.
The monkeys climbed into the
bulldozer engines and chewed the
wires. They let air out of the tyres.

And when the men ran away,
the jaguar ran after them
roaring and snarling.

After that no one could
be found who would risk
being bitten, stung or
clawed in the jungle.

The animals and trees were left in peace. Nothing ever disturbed them.

Afterwards, the other animals called Anthony a hero. He said he wasn't really.

"I couldn't have done it on my own," he said. "A single ant is too small to notice, but when lots of us get together, well, we can move mountains."

What are you going to read next?

Have more adventures with
Horrid Henry,

or save the day with Anthony Ant!

Become a
superhero with Monstar,

float off to
sea with
Algy,

or have your very own Pirates' Picnic.

Grow carrots with

Lottie and Dottie,

make magic with The Witch Dog,

and cast a spell with

The Three Little Magicians.

Enjoy all the Early Readers.